# The Horse That Came To Breakfast

*by **Marilyn D. Anderson***

*illustrated by Dennis E. Miller*

*cover illustration by Estella Lee Hickman*

*To Diana Swanson for all her encouragement*

Published by Willowisp Press, Inc.
401 E. Wilson Bridge Road, Worthington, Ohio 43085

Copyright ©1983 by Willowisp Press, Inc.

Printed in the United States of America

10 9 8 7 6 5 4 3 2

ISBN 0-87406-198-9

# Chapter 1

Loud squealing brakes woke Patty Allen. It sounded as if a car was coming right through the house trailer!

She leaped to her feet and glanced at the clock. It was 6:30 A.M. and barely daylight. Through the window she saw something running away from the road. It was heading for her backyard. Is it a horse? she asked herself.

Patty and her mom came flying out of their rooms at the same time. "What was that?" Mrs. Allen gasped. "It sounded like an accident."

"I don't know, yet," called Patty as she headed for the door.

Still in her pajamas, she stepped out. There in the yard stood a very beautiful horse. It was shaking all over and looked ready to run. If the horse ran away again, it might be hit by a car, Patty thought.

Patty started forward slowly. Maybe she could

get a hold of the horse's halter.

The horse snorted and stepped back, but Patty began to talk to him. "Easy boy, steady fella," she said softly. The horse's copper-colored coat shone. His pale gold mane and tail moved in the light wind.

Patty saw her mother standing in the door and stopped. "Mom," she called softly. "Please bring me a piece of clothesline and an apple."

Her mom was back in a few minutes with both, and she handed them to Patty. The girl held the apple before her and eased forward again. She kept talking, too.

The horse never took his eyes off Patty. He looked ready to run at any minute, but he never did.

Finally, the horse took the apple from Patty as she got hold of him. She fastened the clothesline to his halter and breathed a sigh of relief. She touched the horse and admired him. He was the most beautiful horse she had ever seen.

For years Patty had dreamed of owning a horse, any kind of horse. Every game she played involved horses. Every book she read was about horses. She collected horse statues and horse pictures.

Last summer she had spent almost two months on her cousin Sarah's farm in Ohio. There she had been able to do more than drool over pictures and pretend. Sarah had several horses and Patty had learned to ride well. Sarah's horses had seemed wonderful at the time, but they were nothing like this one. The horse Patty had just found looked like a Thoroughbred.

When her mom came out again, she was fully dressed. She carried a robe for Patty. "Put this on before one of the neighbors sees you," she said.

There was a dreamy look in Patty's eyes. "Oh,

Mom, I wish we could keep him," she sighed.

Mrs. Allen frowned. "You know we can't. This is a valuable horse and he belongs to someone. I'd better call the police right away."

"Not right away," Patty begged. "Just let me pretend for a while that he's mine."

Mrs. Allen shook her head. "I'm sure someone is already very worried about him." Mrs. Allen turned and walked back to the trailer.

Patty knew that her mom was right, but that didn't stop her from dreaming. She put her arms around the horse's neck and hugged him. She petted his sleek hide. She scratched his back.

The horse seemed to like Patty, too. He nuzzled her hair. When she scratched him, he moved closer.

Minutes later, Patty's mom was back. "The riding stable over on Maple Street is missing a horse," she said. "They are going to send someone for him right away."

Patty groaned. "A riding stable? I hoped he belonged to some nice girl. He needs someone to love him."

"I'm sure the riding stable is very nice," Mrs. Allen assured her. "This horse certainly looks well cared for."

"Maybe," said Patty. "But then, why did he run away?"

Mrs. Allen threw up her hands and laughed. "How should I know? I'm not a horse. Anyway, it's not every day we have a horse come to breakfast. You'd better enjoy him while you can."

Enjoy him while you can, Patty said to herself. She hoped no one would come for the horse. The field behind the trailer would be the perfect place to keep him. There was a little barn and the land, covered with tall grass, was all fenced. A horse would enjoy it. A horse would make living in this new town less lonely for her, too.

Patty remembered that weird old Mr. Roberts owned the field. He also owned the barn and the shabby old house down the road. Mr. Roberts hardly ever came out of his house. When he did, it was in the evening. Then, he took his old Ford out just long enough to get groceries. She knew Mr. Roberts wouldn't want a horse in his field.

Patty led the horse to a choice patch of clover. It was wonderful just to stroke his neck and run her hands down his slim legs. She touched his velvety nose and let his whiskers tickle her.

Much too soon, a blond-haired boy came into the

yard. He looked a few years older than Patty and he
carried a rope. The boy stopped to talk to her mom,
first. Then, they came over to Patty and the horse.

"Patty," said her mom. "This is David Wright. His father owns Hilltop Stable."

David smiled at Patty. "I'm sure glad you found Count," he said. "We were afraid he might have gotten hurt."

"What made him run away?" Patty asked suspiciously.

"The other horses pick on him sometimes," David explained. "I think that's why he jumped the fence. We'll put him in a pen of his own during the night from now on."

"That sounds like a good idea," said Patty's mom.

Patty wasn't convinced. "Where does he stay during the day?" she insisted.

"During the day he's either in the barn or out working. Count is one of our best horses to use for riding lessons," said David.

"Oh," was all Patty could say. For a minute, no one spoke. Then Patty said, "He's such a sweet horse. Could I come over sometime and visit him?"

"Sure, come anytime," David agreed. Then he fastened his rope on Count's halter. As he turned to go, he said, "Thanks again for catching our horse. We really appreciate it."

Patty stood and watched the beautiful horse until he was out of sight. She wondered how soon she would be able to see him again.

# Chapter 2

Patty's mom took her on a picnic that weekend. Since her parents' divorce two months earlier, things had been different. Today, her mom was trying hard to be cheerful. Patty tried too, but her heart wasn't in it.

On the way home, her mom suddenly said, "How would you like to go visit the horse you found?"

At once Patty came to life. "Oh, Mom, could we?"

Her mom smiled. "Sure. I think I can find Maple Street, and a stable should be easy to spot."

Maple Street was actually a gravel road. Trees grew thick on each side. At last, they came to a big sign that said "Hilltop Stable, Hunt Lessons Given."

The long driveway had a wooden fence on both sides. It would have been quite impressive with a little paint. The buildings at the end of the lane looked shabby, too, and Patty began to worry. Maybe Count's home wasn't so nice.

Inside the barn, however, things looked much better. All the equipment was neatly stored. The stalls were large and clean. The horses looked fat and happy.

A tall man in riding breeches immediately came up to them. "Hello, I'm Mr. Wright," he said. "Are you interested in taking lessons or would you just like to go for a ride?"

"I just wanted to visit one of your horses," Patty explained. "Count was at our house Wednesday morning."

The man laughed. "So you're the young lady who caught him for us. I want to thank you for that. Count is right over there in the third stall on the left."

Patty's mom had a quick look at Count and went to see the other horses. Patty stayed with her favorite. She wished she could reach him, but he was leaning against the far wall. Only two of her fingers would reach through the wire mesh of the stall, anyway.

Just then David, the boy she'd met Wednesday, came up. "Hi, remember me?" he asked. "I have to saddle this horse right away. He has a rider coming."

"Can I help you?" Patty asked eagerly.

David started to say no. Instead he mumbled, "All right, but don't get in the way."

The boy led the horse into the aisle and tied him with a rope on each side. Then he began to brush Count carefully.

Patty stayed at Count's head and petted him. The horse nuzzled her and seemed happy she was there.

Suddenly, David's father called to him, "Hey, don't bother brushing the horse. Stacy Meadows won't want to wait."

"Okay," David called back. Then he muttered, "That girl is a creep. She can't ride for beans. Dad never let her ride Count before."

David disappeared for a minute. When he returned, he carried a lovely hunt saddle and a bridle with braided reins. Patty had seen pictures of rich people riding saddles like that.

An important-looking girl walked up as David was putting the saddle in place. "So, I get to ride a good-looking horse for once," the girl said. She did not have a friendly smile. "Too bad he's so small for a hunter. Otherwise I'd have my father buy him."

This must be Stacy, thought Patty. She certainly

acts like the brat David described.

Stacy looked down at her own spotless white breeches. She patted the neat braid of dark hair that was wound around her head. Then, she looked at Patty in her faded shorts and T-shirt. "What are you doing here?" she asked. "Do you work here or something?"

David answered for Patty. "No," he said evenly.

"She's just visiting the stable. Is that all right with you?"

Stacy shrugged. "I suppose so. She just looks out of place."

"Miss Meadows," David said coolly. "Your horse is ready. Follow me." With that he set off for the door at a fast walk. It was so fast that Stacy could barely keep up.

Patty followed them at a distance. She didn't want to listen to Stacy anymore. It didn't seem fair that a girl like Stacy could ride Count when she couldn't.

Stacy neatly swung up and put her reins in order. When she was ready, David let go of the horse's head. Then, she was off for an hour on the beautiful Count.

David came back to where Patty was standing. He looked very angry. "I'd love to tell that girl what I think of her. Too bad we need her lesson money so much."

"How much does it cost to take lessons?" Patty wondered.

David explained that each lesson cost fifteen dollars. Ten dollars would rent a horse for an hour.

"Oh," said Patty. Even ten dollars was more than

17

she could spend on riding.

"Well, I'd better get to work," said David. "Come again."

Patty knew that her mom was already in the car, so she started to leave.

As she was walking away, Stacy came trotting over on Count. The dark-haired girl seemed furious. "Get David right now," she ordered.

Patty hesitated. There was no reason for her to obey Stacy. But, she wondered why the girl had come back so soon. If she went to get David, she might find out.

"David, come quick," Patty ran toward him and called. "Stacy wants to see you."

"Yeah, I'll bet," he growled. "She wants someone to wait on her all of the time." He jammed his shovel into the sawdust pile and followed Patty.

Stacy saw him coming. "You know I never ride with a plain snaffle," she fumed. "Put a twisted bit in his mouth right away."

David looked as if he might slap her face. Instead he forced a smile and said, "Oh yeah, I forgot. Just a minute."

He disappeared and returned a minute later with a different bridle. The new bridle was put in place

while Stacy stood by frowning.

When Count was ready, Stacy tossed her head and mounted. As she rode off, she turned to call, "That's an extra ten minutes I have coming."

David muttered to himself, "Thank heaven most of our riders have better hands than she does."

"What do you mean?" Patty wanted to know.

He looked grim. "Count won't be comfortable in that bit. That's because Stacy doesn't know how to control a horse gently."

"Is Count hard to ride?" Patty wondered.

"No," David snorted. "Count is a doll, but that won't last if Stacy keeps riding him. My dad hates giving her lessons. He says she will never be a good rider."

Patty had more questions to ask, but she saw her mom motioning to her. "Oh, I've got to go," she told David.

"Remember, we'd be glad to have you anytime," he said.

On the way home her mom said, "I suppose you will want to walk over here every day to check on Count. I don't want you to become a pest. Don't go over again unless I take you."

"But, Mom," Patty objected. "David said I was

welcomed, that they'd be glad to have me."

"What else could he say?" her mother insisted. "I'll bet he was glad to have you leave him alone."

This time Patty didn't answer. She couldn't agree to stay away from Count. She would keep track of the horse and of Stacy, too.

# Chapter 3

Patty thought about Count the whole next day. She was dying to go visit him again, but her mom wouldn't like that. Patty remembered that David had said the horse went out at night. Maybe she could just pat him through the fence without bothering anyone.

Early the next morning Patty started off toward Maple Street. At last, she could see horses grazing on the other side of the trees. Count was in a pen all by himself and he wasn't far from the road.

Patty looked around. She didn't want anyone to watch her. Quickly, she slipped into the trees and went over to the fence. She called softly to Count.

The gelding looked up. He seemed puzzled. When Patty called again, he walked toward the sound of her voice. His big brown eyes looked at her hopefully.

"Looking for an apple?" she teased. "Well, here it is."

Count carefully took the apple. He slowly chewed it and looked for more.

"That's all," Patty told him. "But, I will scratch your back if you come closer."

He seemed to understand because he moved closer to the fence. Patty scratched him all over. When she began to stroke his face, she found red marks at the sides of his mouth. She wondered if they were from Stacy's rough hands on the reins.

Suddenly, Patty heard a voice calling the horses. Someone was coming from the barn. She slipped back into the trees to watch.

David's father was at the gate calling, "Come, Count. Time to go in."

Then Patty heard him say, "Stacy wants you for her lesson today. Got to get you ready."

Count saw the pail of grain in Mr. Wright's hand and went to him. In a few minutes they were out of sight.

Darn it, Stacy is going to ride him again, Patty said to herself. I want to see that.

She walked farther down the road. She could see that the road ran on two sides of the stable property. The area for giving lessons seemed to be next to the road and the trees, too. Maybe I could watch the whole lesson without being seen, she muttered to herself.

After a while three horses and their riders came into view. Each rider wore tall black boots and a black velvet cap. There was Stacy on Count. He was much prettier than the other dark-colored horses.

Mr. Wright first had the riders circle the ring at a walk. The other riders quietly walked along, but not Stacy. She was fussing with Count's reins and she kicked him several times.

Mr. Wright saw Stacy and said, "What are you trying to do?"

"I'm trying to teach this horse some manners," she said crossly. "He keeps wanting to put his head down."

"Then let him put it down," said Mr. Wright. "We always let our horses warm up with their heads down. That makes their backs looser for the rest of the lesson. Now, leave his mouth alone and give him some rein." Stacy pouted. She tossed her head and gave Count only a few more inches of rein.

Mr. Wright turned to the other riders and said, "Yes, Rosie, that looks very good. Kim, don't let him fall asleep." He looked at Stacy again and yelled, "Stacy, give him more rein!"

"But, he's pulling on my hands," Stacy argued.

"Well, don't hold him so tight," Mr. Wright snapped.

Patty felt sorry for Count. If he weren't so pretty, Stacy wouldn't insist on riding him.

The instructor began to give directions to the first rider in line. "Rosie, you are going to trot to the end of the line," he told her. "When I say go, begin to post."

The girl's fat pony was lazy. She had to kick hard to make him trot. Then, she began to stand up and down in her stirrups.

"Very nice," said Mr. Wright. "Now, Kim, let's see you do the same thing."

Kim's chocolate-colored horse was eager to trot. He wanted to catch Rosie's pony. However, Kim was not ready to start so quickly. Her posting looked very uneven.

"You're not posting fast enough," Mr. Wright called to her. "Up, down, up, down. That's better."

Then, it was Count's turn. The horse looked eager to go if Stacy would just let him. Instead, she hauled on her reins and booted him. The horse's head came up and he broke into a frantic canter.

"Stacy," yelled Mr. Wright. "Stop! You must

learn to be more gentle. You scared that poor horse to death. Try it again and leave the reins alone."

Stacy muttered and fussed, but she was more gentle. This time Count moved off in a nice trot. Stacy bounced for a while, but she finally picked up the posting motion.

"That's better," said Mr. Wright. He sounded relieved. "Now, everyone trot together. "Up, down, up, down, heels down, elbows back . . ."

The class posted the trot for several times around the ring. Then they trotted in the other direction. They were told to follow the horse's outside shoulder as they moved. At last it was time to canter.

Stacy waited until the other horses were far ahead. Count was eager to catch up. She sent him off very fast and passed the other horses.

"Walk," demanded Mr. Wright in a very loud voice. "This is not a horse race. It takes skill to make a horse canter slowly."

"All right, all right," Stacy interrupted. "Let's go again."

Through clenched teeth, Mr. Wright said, "You may try it again if you will follow directions. Since you are in the lead now, canter just to the end of the line."

Now that he was in the lead, Count was not so eager to go. Stacy hauled on his mouth and madly kicked. The horse got very upset and began to throw his head in the air. Stacy was nearly hit in the face.

The girl squealed in surprise. "Did you see that?" she demanded. "Next time I want this horse's head tied down."

Mr. Wright's face was turning red. "That will not be necessary. All you need are quieter hands. Let me ride the horse, please."

Stacy angrily slid off. As she did there was a

stubborn look on her face.

Mr. Wright eased himself onto Count's back. He didn't bother to lengthen the stirrups because he didn't need them. Gently, he asked Count to tuck in his nose. He had the horse walk a short distance. Then, Count was cantering without any fuss. If there was any signal from the rider, Patty hadn't seen it.

"Well," Stacy snapped, "you should be able to do it. You are the instructor."

As Mr. Wright slid off, Stacy grabbed the reins from his hands. She hauled herself back onto Count and took a very short hold on his reins. Without warning she kicked him with both feet and yelled "yeah."

The startled horse bounded into a gallop. Stacy went a short way and yanked him to a stop. "See," she bragged. "I knew how to get a canter all along. I just wanted to see if you did."

"This lesson is over," stormed Mr. Wright. "Stacy will walk back to the barn."

When they were gone Patty felt like crying. How could Count survive with Stacy riding him? she thought. He must be very unhappy. Patty hoped Stacy would get tired of the horse, soon.

# Chapter 4

It was a tense morning for Patty. Her mom insisted that she take swimming lessons. She hadn't swum in ages. She barely remembered how to do the dog paddle.

Patty had an old, brown swimsuit. The color was all washed out and she'd almost outgrown it. It was going to be awful facing a lot of new kids in the old suit, she felt.

Poor Count would be looking for his apple, too. For a week now Patty had been visiting him early in the morning. Swimming lessons started at 8:30 A.M. A walk to Maple Street would be impossible.

Patty thought about disappointing Count all the way to the pool. He was so sweet and patient. When beginners rode him, he was very gentle. When the better riders rode him, he seemed to fly over the jumps. Only one rider had trouble with him. That rider was Stacy Meadows.

There was no one at the pool but the teachers when Patty got there. She changed into her suit and came out to look around. A lady took Patty's name and told her where the intermediates would be.

It wasn't long before the other kids began to arrive. Only one person out of all the kids looked familiar. Stacy Meadows was in the intermediate class, too.

Stacy looked great as usual. She wore a bright red suit that fit her perfectly. Her dark hair was in French braids and she had a gorgeous tan.

Patty tried not to look at Stacy. Instead, she turned to the girl on her other side. "Hi, I'm Patty Allen. What's your name?" she asked.

"I'm Nicki Pierson," the curly-headed girl answered. "Are you as scared as I am? I don't know any of the stuff that intermediates have to do."

"I don't either," said Patty. "But, I hope I learn quickly "

Just then a voice behind Patty said, "Nicki, I haven't seen you since school let out. Where have you been?"

Patty turned and found herself face to face with Stacy. Quickly, she looked away again.

Nicki said, "Oh, around."

Stacy ignored Patty. "Well, I've called your house several times. Your mother always says that you're busy." Then she stared at Patty. "Haven't I

seen you somewhere before?" she asked. "It couldn't have been here. You certainly don't have a tan."

Patty tried to sound cheerful. "Uh, sure, you saw me at Hilltop Stable a few weeks ago."

"Oh, now I remember," Stacy said in sort of a bored tone. "You were just visiting, I believe."

Nicki interrupted, "Do you ride, Patty? I've only done it once or twice, but it sure is fun," she said.

"Before I moved here I rode my cousin's horse," said Patty.

"Oh," snorted Stacy. "You didn't take lessons or anything, right?"

"Right," Patty had to agree.

"Well," bragged Stacy, "I take lessons once a week and sometimes I go riding on my own. I ride this gorgeous horse named Count. My instructor says I'm going to be jumping soon."

Nicki seemed impressed. "That sounds terrific," she said. "I'd love to see you do it sometime."

Patty wanted to tell Nicki that she knew Stacy was lying. And she wanted to tell that brat, Stacy, what a terrible rider she was, too. But, she could not let Stacy know that her lessons had been watched.

When Patty didn't answer Stacy went on, trying to sound important. "I think my father may buy

Count. The horse needs a lot of work, of course. We'd probably have to have him retrained."

Patty could hardly control her tongue. Why would Stacy want to buy a hunter? She can't even canter correctly. It would be awful for Count if Stacy bought him, Patty thought.

Stacy was staring at Patty now. She expected Patty to be impressed. She looked so sure of herself that Patty wanted to shock her.

At last Patty said, "Do you think you're ready for jumping? That takes a really good rider, you know."

Stacy's eyes narrowed in anger. "I am a very good rider and don't you forget it. What do you know about it anyway? You've never even taken lessons." With that she turned and stalked off.

Nicki gave a low whistle. "You sure ruffled her feathers," she whispered. "No one ever questions Stacy's bragging. That makes her get nasty. She thinks everyone is impressed by her stories."

Patty was surprised. "You mean, you didn't believe what she said?"

Nicki laughed. "Why do you think I was always busy when Stacy called? I went to the stables with her once. She never even let me on the horse. All she did was show off. I know what kind of a rider she is and I'll bet her horse is a plug, too."

"That one part of her story is true," Patty objected. "Count is the most beautiful horse there ever was. He jumps beautifully. I just hope and pray she doesn't buy him."

Nicki looked at her. "How do you know so much about the horse?"

"He got loose and came to my house one morning. Ever since, I've wished I had the money to ride him," Patty explained.

"Hmmmmm," said Nicki. "I suppose you could start picking up aluminum cans along the road," she said. Then she laughed at her own joke.

Patty knew Nicki was teasing, but the idea didn't sound so dumb to her. In fact, it might be worth a try.

Just then the swimming teacher called, "Intermediates into the water, please."

From then on Patty was too busy to worry about anything but swimming. It was hard work for her and she did want to do well.

On the way home Patty started looking for cans. If she could find enough she might be able to get enough money to ride Count someday.

# Chapter 5

Patty found three aluminum cans on the way home from swimming. After lunch she looked until she found seven more. It would take a long time to earn ten dollars this way. Then she thought, Maybe I could find enough to earn five dollars this week. I wonder if the stable would let me rent Count for half an hour. It was an exciting thought.

By 2:00 P.M. Wednesday, Patty had her five dollars. It helped that she had saved some allowance. She put all of the money in her pocket and nervously headed toward Maple Street.

When Patty got to the stable, she found it very quiet. The horses were asleep in their stalls. It seemed as if no one was around. She was about to call to Count when David saw her.

"Hi, Patty. What are you doing here?" he said in surprise.

Patty didn't know what to say. He probably

wouldn't let her ride for just five dollars. "I was sort of wondering . . ." she stammered. "That is, I've been saving my money . . . Uh, could I rent a horse for a half hour?" she finished in a rush.

For a minute it looked as if David might laugh. But finally, he said, "Well, we normally don't do that, but business is slow today. Why not?"

Patty's eyes lit up. "Oh, terrific!" she exploded. "I'm so excited that I can hardly wait."

"Is that so?" David teased. "Then I guess I had better hurry and saddle Poncho the pony."

For a minute Patty was afraid he was serious. Would he really make her ride a pony? Then, she realized he was teasing. "Could I ride Count instead?" she asked politely.

"Of course," he grinned. "The customer is always right." He brought a saddle and Count was ready in no time. Then he asked, "Do you know anything about riding, Patty?"

"Some," she nervously answered. "I've never been on an English saddle. Most of my riding has been bareback."

David looked pleased. "If you can stay on bareback I think you will do all right with this saddle. Just remember to use one hand on each rein. It's

not like riding a western horse."

Patty nodded. She was too excited to talk just
then. She took both reins in one hand and swung
up. The stirrups were just long enough and the

saddle was comfortable. She gave David a smile and started off.

It was heaven to be on an eager horse like Count. Sarah's horses had always been lazy about leaving the barn. Count seemed to enjoy the trails. They trotted and cantered and jumped low logs. When they came to a little stream, Patty let him play in the water. She let him graze for a few minutes while she checked the girth. Then, they trotted and cantered some more. The half hour was over much too quickly.

"How was it?" David asked as he took Count from her.

Patty was beaming. "He's wonderful," she sighed. "I wish I could afford to do this every day."

"I wish you could, too," David chuckled. "We need the money." Then he grew more serious as he added, "Count seems happier with you than he does with Stacy."

Patty frowned. "Stacy says her father might buy Count. That's not true, is it? I mean, your father wouldn't sell him to someone like her, would he?"

David shrugged. "I don't know. We need the money pretty bad. Dad might not have any choice."

"Really?" gulped Patty. "Do you think Stacy's

dad would decide to buy him soon?"

"No," said David, shaking his head. "I don't think Mr. Meadows will buy her a hunter until she's done some jumping. The way she rides that could be quite a while."

Patty dared to breathe again. "Good," she sighed. "Maybe, soon, things will look up for you and your dad and you won't have to sell Count after all."

On the way home Patty couldn't help thinking how wonderful it would be if she could buy Count. But, she knew that would never be possible. The best she could hope for would be to ride him as often as she could get the money.

She looked for cans again that night. She stashed them in the broom closet.

Her mom was sitting in the easy chair watching TV when Patty came in. When she saw Patty, she said, "What have you been up to all evening?"

"I just went for a walk," Patty fibbed. She was afraid her mom might tell her again, to stay away from Hilltop Stable.

Her mom said no more and Patty sat down to watch TV. But, she couldn't get interested in it. Instead, her mind raced to think of new ways to earn riding money.

The next day Patty was searching along a side road when she noticed an old lady watching her. After a while, the woman called to her, "Come over here, please. I want to talk to you."

Patty hesitated. The woman was a stranger. But Patty decided the old lady was probably just lonesome, so she went over.

"I've been watching you for a long time," said the woman. "You are a hard worker."

"I'm trying to earn enough money to ride a certain horse at Hilltop Stable," Patty explained.

"That's nice," the woman nodded. "I've always liked horses. You know, I have some jobs around here that need doing. Could I hire you?"

Patty was surprised. She'd never thought of working for someone. What kind of job could I do? she asked herself.

The woman looked sad. "My strawberries need weeding, but my back is sore. Do you think you could do that for me?"

Patty brightened. "Sure, I'm good at weeding," she agreed.

"Well good," said the woman with a big smile. "My name is Mrs. Bex. What's yours?"

"Patty Allen."

"Hello, Patty Allen," said Mrs. Bex. "If you will come this way, I'll get you started." She led the way to her neat little garden.

The strawberry patch was the biggest part of the garden. Patty pulled weeds until she was sweaty and dirty, but she was proud of what she had done.

At last, Mrs. Bex brought a glass of lemonade and

a bag of aluminum cans. "You did a very good job," she said, handing Patty the lemonade. "I think you deserve two dollars. Maybe you would like these cans, too."

Patty beamed. So far today she had earned almost four dollars. She might be able to ride Count again, soon. She sipped her lemonade slowly and asked, "Do you have any more jobs around here for me to do?"

"Not today," said Mrs. Bex in a kindly way. "But do check with me next Tuesday. I think my lawn will need mowing then."

* * * * * *

On Friday the strap on Patty's old swimsuit broke during the middle of class. There was nothing she could do about it except stand there and hold the broken strap.

At last, one of the teachers brought her a big safety pin. Patty had to wear that the rest of class.

After school Patty thought about how much she needed a new suit. She couldn't go back to class with a safety pin holding it together. How could she learn to swim if she had to worry about her dumb strap? Maybe Mom would get her a new suit before Monday.

While walking home Patty decided to search for cans along the rode by the stable. It was lucky she had brought a bag because there were lots of them to find. She was so busy looking at the ground that before she knew it she was next to the Hilltop property.

Suddenly, a voice said, "Is that Miss Safety Pins from swimming class? I do believe she's picking up cans."

Patty looked up in horror. There was Stacy and another girl from class staring at her.

"Think you'll find enough for a new suit?" Stacy laughed.

Patty wished she were dead. She grabbed her cans and ran. It was a long time before she stopped hearing Stacy's laughter.

As soon as Mom got home that night Patty ran to tell her about the broken strap and the safety pin. She didn't tell her about the can money, however.

"Can I have a new suit, Mom?" she begged. "Mine is way too small, the color is all gone and it's falling apart."

Mom looked sad. She didn't answer right away. At last she said, "No, I'll just have to fix your old suit. I can't write any more checks this week."

"Can't we charge it?" Patty wailed.

"No," Mom said firmly. "I cut the credit cards and threw them away when your father and I decided to split up."

Patty turned and ran to her room sobbing. It wasn't her fault her mom and dad had gotten a divorce. Why did she have to be the poorest kid in town? She just had to have a new suit.

She thought about what Stacy had said. She

wondered if she really could earn enough money to buy a new swimsuit. On second thought, Patty knew she could swing it.

But, she remembered her wonderful afternoon on Count, too. If she spent all her money on a swimsuit, she wouldn't be able to ride Count for a long time.

Maybe Mom could fix the swimsuit strap, she thought.

# Chapter 6

By Saturday, Patty had decided that Count was more important than any swimsuit. She wanted to ride him today, but the stable would be too busy for any five-dollar rides.

She did pay Count an early morning visit. The horse nickered as soon as he saw Patty and came right over for his apple. Then, he moved closer to the fence to be scratched. Patty told Count how much she had missed him.

She saw the barn door open. Mr. Wright walked over to the fence and called to Count. She slipped back into the trees and watched until Count was out of sight. The weekend riders rode the trails. There was no point in hanging around.

Swimming lessons on Monday were just as terrible as Patty had feared. Mrs. Allen had nicely

repaired the strap, but still Stacy teased her about it. "Hey, Safety Pins," the brat called out as soon as she saw Patty.

Patty tried to ignore her. She stared at the pool.

"I see you didn't find enough cans to buy a new suit," Stacy called even louder. "That's too bad. Your old one is a mess."

Patty kept staring at the pool. She hoped Stacy would stop teasing her soon. When it grew quiet Patty dared to look around. She saw a whole group of girls listening to Stacy. It wasn't hard for her to guess why they were giggling.

After class Nicki told her that Stacy had been bragging again. Stacy claimed she had jumped over a two-foot log in the woods. She planned to force Mr. Wright into letting her jump during lessons.

"What a fool," Patty fumed. "Mr. Wright won't let her jump until she's good enough. It would be too dangerous."

Nicki looked thoughtfully at Patty and sighed, "I don't know. That girl seems to always get what she wants."

"I wonder if she will be riding this afternoon," Patty said.

Nicki shook her head. "Stacy is going shopping

with her mother today. They will be gone until late afternoon."

"Good," said Patty. "I've just got to talk to someone about this."

* * * * * *

David was by himself when Patty got to Hilltop. He grinned at her and said, "We're in luck. Stacy isn't coming today."

"I'll say," Patty agreed. "Lately, she's been just awful to me."

"She's been a pain around here, too," he nodded. "Now she wants Dad to let her start jumping."

Patty groaned. "On Count, I suppose. The poor horse will get all messed up if she does that. Can't your dad refuse?"

"She's threatening to go to some other stable if she can't jump here," David said grimly. "I told you that we need her money and Count is our safest jumper."

"I hope she falls on her head," Patty said angrily. "Maybe then she won't want to buy Count."

"Now wait a minute," David objected. "We don't want to get sued."

"But, it would be her fault," Patty reminded him.

Then she said, "Let's forget about Stacy. I've got five dollars. Can I ride Count?"

"Sure, I'll get him for you," David agreed.

That afternoon was just as wonderful as her first ride on Count. They splashed through streams and cantered along the winding trails. They jumped logs and had a great time. The half hour was over too soon.

When Patty returned, David said, "Is your time up already? I hadn't noticed."

Patty smiled shyly. "You know it is."

"Did you have a good time?" he asked.

"Oh, yes," said Patty. "We jumped a bunch of logs today. Count just floats over them."

David looked interested. "He does, eh? How about showing me?" he asked as he brought a safety helmet.

Patty was surprised. She wasn't paying for any jumping lessons. What will David think of my riding? she wondered. Oh well, I'd love to have a few more minutes on Count.

David had her trot around the arena before jumping. Then he said, "Now canter easy and put him over that little crossed-rail jump."

Patty put Count smoothly into a canter and

headed for the jump. Although it wasn't very high, she rose in her stirrups to meet Count's body. His jumping was effortless.

"Not bad," called David. "You naturally have good timing and balance. Of course, your elbows would look better if you didn't flap them."

Patty blushed. She would remember to keep her elbows in next time, if there was a next time.

"Try the double bars on the other side now," David was calling. "They're just a little higher."

Patty was delighted. This was fun. She brought Count squarely to the jump. Her hands and body followed the horse up and over. She even remembered to keep her elbows in.

"Very good," David cheered. "I wish you could afford to take lessons from my father. You've really got talent."

"Do you really think so?" Patty beamed. "I'd give anything to be able to take jumping lessons, especially on Count."

David looked thoughtful. "We never have much business on Mondays," he told her. "Maybe I could give you a few pointers if you were to help me clean stalls."

"Gee, that sounds wonderful," Patty bubbled.

"I'd love to help clean stalls. I'll be here for sure next Monday."

"Now, take it easy. I said 'maybe,' " he reminded her. "I can't promise anything. You would have to come up with the five dollars as usual."

"Oh, I'll have the money, and I know we'll be able to do it," she said eagerly.

The next afternoon Patty mowed Mrs. Bex's lawn. She searched everywhere for cans that evening and the next afternoon. She wanted to be sure to have enough money to ride Count again during the week as well as on Monday.

Thursday morning at swimming lessons Patty kept her ears tuned to Stacy. She figured that if Stacy wasn't riding today, she was.

"I've had two jumping lessons already," she heard Stacy say.

Patty's heart wanted to stop. Stacy wasn't wasting any time. She must have taken two lessons in two days. Poor Count.

Stacy went on. "My dad is so proud of me that he's coming to watch my lessons this afternoon. He's always said that he would buy me a horse when I could jump. I'm going to jump higher today so he'll be really impressed."

By now Patty was feeling sick. If Mr. Meadows was coming this afternoon, he must be serious about buying Count. The horse might be sold before Patty ever rode him again.

# Chapter 7

Patty gulped down her lunch and raced to her secret spot next to the lesson arena. It would be awful watching Stacy jump Count, but she couldn't stay away. She was shaking all over as she waited.

This time Stacy was the only student. Mr. Wright was talking to a fat man in golf clothes. Patty figured the fat man must be Stacy's father.

Mr. Meadows said, "I've been waiting to see Stacy jump for a long time. I hope she will be ready for some shows by fall."

"Well, she's just starting," Mr. Wright said in a flat tone. "I doubt she will be ready for a while."

Mr. Meadows continued with confidence. "I'm sure that with the right horse, it won't take her long to get the hang of it. This horse she's riding today is certainly a handsome beast."

"Yes, Count is one of our nicest horses," Mr. Wright admitted. "He jumps beautifully."

"Well then," said Mr. Meadows. "Let's get on with the lesson. I haven't got all day."

Mr. Wright had Stacy warm up Count with an easy posting trot. She was on her best behavior, so far. Maybe she didn't want Mr. Wright to yell at her in front of her father.

Mr. Meadows proudly smiled as Stacy trotted by him. He smiled even wider when she began to canter.

Finally, Mr. Wright said she could try some low jumps. He certainly didn't look very happy.

Patty could see that Count was jumping in spite of Stacy. The girl seemed to lurch forward whenever the horse's body went up. To her the reins were handles to grab for balance.

Mr. Wright suggested that she grab some of Count's mane to steady herself. He explained that the horse needed his head for balance. However, Stacy was too proud for that, and Count began to hesitate at the jumps.

Mr. Meadows was frowning now. "The horse doesn't seem very interested in jumping to me," he said. "I'd say he wouldn't be able to jump much higher."

Stacy looked over at her father. A determined

look crossed her face. She stared at the bigger jumps that were used for more advanced students. All at once she hit Count with both heels and yelled.

The startled horse leaped forward toward one of the highest jumps. Patty saw he was going over it although Stacy was badly off balance.

Then, just as the horse left the ground, Stacy panicked. She grabbed at the reins and tried to stay on. Instead, she pulled Count's head around to the left and he completely lost his balance. His body twisted in midair. He fell on a broken, wooden bar.

Stacy bounced clear and started to howl. Count merely gave a squeal of pain and lay still.

Patty leaped from her hiding place and raced to the horse. The men were busy with Stacy. Count was badly bleeding from his chest. Patty pressed her hand down hard over the huge cut and she managed to reduce the flow of blood. Count's eyes were wild now. He lay gasping for air.

"My head hurts. I won't ever ride that dumb horse again," Stacy sobbed.

In a loud voice Mr. Meadows threatened, "I'll sue this crummy stable. You haven't heard the last of this." Minutes later he and his noisy daughter were gone.

Then, Mr. Wright came over to help Patty. "Where did you come from?" he demanded at first. Then, without waiting for an answer, he added, "Let me see how bad it is."

Patty moved her hand and let him see the huge gash. Suddenly, she saw how the bridle was cutting into Count's throat. She quickly undid the bridle and the girth on the saddle. Then, she returned to Mr. Wright's elbow.

"Is he going to be all right?" she asked in a frightened voice.

"I think so," Mr. Wright told her. "But, where did you come from?" he remembered.

Patty stammered. "Well, I was just passing by, and I stopped to watch the lesson . . ."

"Good," interrupted Mr. Wright. "I might need you to tell what you saw if Mr. Meadows does try to sue me."

Patty nodded. "I saw the whole thing. It was all Stacy's fault. Do you think we should call a vet?"

"I'm sure that David has taken care of that by now," said Mr. Wright. "He said he was going to keep an eye on this lesson."

"I love Count so much that I just can't stand to see him hurt like this," she said sadly.

Mr. Wright looked strangely at her. "What? How come you're so attached to my horse?"

Patty decided to confess everything. "I've been spying on Count ever since he came over to my house. I've ridden him, too."

"Here comes the vet," interrupted Mr. Wright. "David, how's Stacy?"

"She's not hurt," David growled. "She was combing her hair as they left. How's the horse?"

"I think he'll need some stitches at least," Mr. Wright said grimly.

The vet bent over Count and looked at the huge wound. "Good thing the horse is staying quiet," he said. "It would have been much worse for him if he had struggled."

He gave Count a shot and put some powder in the wound. Then, he began to stitch the pieces of flesh back together. Patty watched the needle go through the bloody hide.

When the vet finished, he said, "Let's get this horse on his feet within the next hour. Someone should stay with him until then."

"I want to," Patty volunteered.

"I'll stay too," David offered.

"Good," said Mr. Wright. "I've got to find out for sure about Stacy and call my insurance man. If you'll come with me, Dr. Wilson, I'll write you a check."

When the men had gone, David said angrily, "That dumb Stacy. Too bad Count has to suffer for her stupidity."

"What will happen to him now?" Patty wondered.

"That's hard to say," David answered. "That wound will take a long time to heal. He won't make much money for us in this condition."

"At least Stacy won't want him now, will she?"

Patty asked hopefully.

"I should say not," David snorted. "The Meadows think the whole accident was the horse's fault."

"How long will it take for Count to be well?" Patty wondered.

David shrugged. "A few months, I suppose. If we can keep him that long, I guess he'll be useful again by then."

"What do you mean, 'if you can keep him?'" Patty asked.

David hesitated. "This stable may not be open much longer. Dad has been talking to a possible buyer. If they make a deal, all the horses will have to be sold right away."

"How soon?" gasped Patty.

"That depends on the buyer," David answered. "The worst part is that no one is going to buy Count in this condition."

"What would happen to him then?" she demanded.

"Since no one will want a horse that has a wounded chest and is probably lame, he may have to be put to sleep," he said.

"Put to sleep?" Patty almost screamed. "There must be someone who will give him a chance to get better."

"Maybe, and I'm sure Dad will look before he does anything hasty," David said evenly.

Patty was too upset to talk anymore.

After a while they helped Count to his feet and brought him back to the barn. When he was comfortable Patty went home and worried about the horse.

# Chapter 8

Friday was the last day of swimming lessons. Patty couldn't think about going. She had to know how Count was.

Mr. Wright and the veterinarian were in the horse's stall when she got to Hilltop. David was busy showing the other horses to a young couple.

Patty slipped into Count's stall and tried to see around the men. She thought the horse looked more alert this morning. He was even eating. Only his swollen chest looked frightening.

"Too bad you need to sell this horse now," the vet was saying. "That gash is going to take time to heal."

Mr. Wright nodded. "Yesterday he was worth about $2000. Today he wouldn't bring $500. I'd probably have to sell him by the pound."

"Wouldn't this fellow who bought the stable keep him for a while?" the vet suggested.

"No, he needs all these stalls," Mr. Wright explained. "Besides, I could barely afford a normal boarding bill. Extra care would get expensive."

Patty could barely believe her ears. The stable was already sold. She hadn't thought it would happen so fast.

"That's true," the vet was saying. "The wound must be kept clean. This horse should be by himself and away from flies."

Patty was glad to see the men go. She offered Count his apple, and he took it eagerly. "You can't be too sick if you're that hungry," she told him.

Then David joined her. He looked very unhappy as he said, "I guess that's the end of Hilltop Stable for us."

"I heard that your dad sold the place," she said softly.

"Yeah, Dad closed the deal last night," he told her. "The people that are here now will probably buy the horses. I hope they do because we have to be out in a week."

Patty stiffened. "A week? Will they buy Count, too?"

David looked at the ground. "No," he said softly. "I asked them."

"Oh, gosh," Patty realized. "Then we've got to find a place for him right away."

"The sooner the better," the boy agreed. "It would be a shame for a young horse like Count to end up as dog food."

Patty was so close to crying that she could do no more than nod. She would have to think of something. If she owned the field behind the house trailer, she could take Count herself. It would be a joy to nurse him back to health. But, old Mr. Roberts owned the field. She didn't think he would let Count stay there. But, maybe the old man needed money. If Mr. Wright offered him some rent, Mr. Roberts might go for the idea. There could be no harm in trying.

When Patty mentioned the idea to Mr. Wright, he listened thoughtfully. "Thank you for the idea," he said doubtfully. "I don't have much hope it will work out. Mr. Roberts doesn't have a phone. He might not even talk to me."

"Well, will you at least try?" she begged.

"Yes, it is worth a try," he agreed.

The next day Patty learned that the old man had refused to even answer his door. Mr. Wright said he didn't have any more time to waste on the hermit.

Patty's heart sank. Unless she could talk to Mr. Roberts, Count's future looked grim.

Mr. Roberts' house looked so spooky that it took all of Patty's courage to knock on the door. The curtains of the shabby old house were drawn. The lawn badly needed mowing.

No one answered Patty's knocks for a long time, but she kept trying. She saw the curtains move. She decided to try again.

The door opened a crack and a face peeked out. "What do you want?" the rusty voice demanded.

"Uh, I'm your neighbor, Patty Allen. I wanted to talk to you about . . ." Patty began excitedly.

"Nothing to talk about," the old man muttered, and he closed the door with a bang.

That made Patty angry. Why wouldn't he talk to her? Did he think she was going to hurt him? He just had to listen. Count was depending on her.

Patty was muttering to herself as she walked home. "I wish I could just wait until he comes out for groceries. I'd get him then. But, that could take days. Doesn't that old man have any friends in town? There must be someone who knows how to reach him."

Then Patty thought of Mrs. Bex. The old woman

had lived around here for a long time. She and Mr. Roberts had to be about the same age.

Patty ran all the way to Mrs. Bex's house and pounded on the door. The old lady seemed surprised to see her. "Well, well, come in," she bubbled. "You look all upset. Won't you sit down and tell me about it?"

"It's about Mr. Roberts who lives next to us," Patty panted. "What's the matter with him?"

Mrs. Bex grew very serious. "What's he done?"

"Oh, he hasn't done anything," Patty assured her. "I just went over there to ask him something important. He slammed the door in my face."

"That doesn't surprise me," Mrs. Bex sighed. "Fred has shut himself up in that house for too long. I think he's afraid of people now."

Quickly, Patty explained about Count's accident. She told Mrs. Bex how much the horse needed to stay in Mr. Roberts' pasture. "How can I get him to listen to me?" she finished.

Mrs. Bex didn't answer for several minutes. At last she said, "This is just what Fred needs. He kept a lovely horse in that pasture for years. Then one day it got tangled in the barbed wire and slowly bled to death. Fred was never the same after that."

Patty gasped. "Oh, how awful!"

"Yes," Mrs. Bex continued, "Fred never married and that horse was all he had." Suddenly, the old lady grabbed her purse and headed for the door. "Come on," she said. "I'm going over there with you. I don't think he will throw me out."

Patty gave a little cheer and ran to keep up.

*  *  *  *  *  *

Mrs. Bex had to knock on the door several times, too. When the curtains parted a little, they could see a face peeking out. Finally, the door opened a crack.

Mrs. Bex put her foot in the crack and said, "Fred, I haven't seen you in a long time. Remember me? I'm Lucy Bex."

Mr. Roberts' mouth dropped open. "Lucy Bex?" he wondered. "You're too old to be Lucy Bex."

"It's been a long time, Fred," she said softly. "Won't you come out and talk to me?"

Mr. Roberts nervously looked around and stayed where he was. "I don't know," he croaked. "I don't like to visit much anymore."

"It's very important, Fred," she insisted. "A life

depends on you. You must listen to what this girl has to say."

The old man stared at Patty. He looked doubtful. "What do you mean a life depends on me?"

"It's a horse, Mr. Roberts," Patty stammered. "A wonderful horse may be sold for dog food if you can't help us."

"A horse?" he muttered. "I don't want to hear about it." He would have closed the door if it hadn't been for Mrs. Bex's foot.

Patty went on desperately. "The horse's name is Count and he's hurt. The owner can't keep him. No one will buy him with a big gash in his chest."

The old man was quiet. Patty thought the old man had forgotten all about her when he said, "How did the horse get hurt?"

So he was interested! That gave Patty hope. "A stupid girl tried to jump him higher than she should have. Count landed on a sharp board," she went on breathlessly. "Could we keep him in your pasture until he's healed?"

The old man looked upset now. "One horse died in that pasture. That's enough," he said in a strange voice.

"This horse isn't going to die," Patty protested.

"The horse will be just fine if we can help him."

"Fred, you aren't using that pasture. It wouldn't hurt to let the girl put a horse in there," Mrs. Bex added.

Mr. Roberts seemed to be fighting some battle within himself. At last he said, "All right, you can put the horse in my field, but don't expect me to help you with him."

"Oh, thank you," Patty exploded. "I'll be glad to take care of him by myself."

Mrs. Bex was beaming. "Yes, thank you, Fred. We won't bother you anymore." As she finished, she pulled her foot back out of the door.

Patty looked back at the old man as they walked away. She noticed that he hadn't closed his door. In fact, he was still watching them with an odd look on his face.

Mrs. Bex happily bubbled all the way back to her house. Patty could see that the old lady was quite pleased with herself. "What a good idea this was," she said over and over again. "This will help Fred more than it does the horse." Patty was too happy to talk.

As Patty was leaving, Mrs. Bex asked, "Have you told your mother about all of this?"

Patty gave a little start. "No, I haven't," she had to admit. Her mom would be home in an hour or so, and she might not be pleased. Patty had been told to stay away from the stable. Here she was plotting to adopt one of its horses instead.

# Chapter 9

Patty nervously waited for her mom's car to pull in the driveway. When Patty went to meet her, Mrs. Allen began to get suspicious.

"What are you up to?" her mother asked. "You never come out to meet me unless you want something."

Patty just shook her head and made her mom sit down in the living room before she began to explain. Before she had finished, her mom was frowning.

"Oh, Patty, how did you get involved in all this?" her mother sighed. "I told you not to bother the people at the stable. Now I find out that you did bother them. You've gotten Mrs. Bex and poor old Mr. Roberts all excited, too."

Patty was worried. Maybe her mom wouldn't let her take Count after all. "Mom," she said quickly. "Mrs. Bex didn't mind helping me. It was her idea to go over to Mr. Roberts' house. She said this was just what he needed."

Mrs. Allen looked doubtful. "I wonder why she said that. I'd say that poor old man just wants to be left alone."

Patty was getting more and more worried. Her mom had too many questions. "I don't know why she said that," the girl said desperately. "I do know that he lost a horse he loved a long time ago."

"What would happen when the horse is well?" Mom went on.

Patty had tried not to think about that part. She hesitated. "I guess Mr. Wright will sell him," she admitted.

"Would you be able to give him up, then?" her mom demanded. "It might be easier to just forget about him now."

"Mom, I'm not the one that matters," Patty said bravely. "Count deserves to get well and live a useful life again."

It seemed that Mrs. Allen had run out of questions for a while. At last she said, "You will try to be careful around that horse, won't you?"

Patty stared at her for a minute. She wondered if she had heard right. "Does this mean that I can do it?" she asked in a puzzled way.

Mrs. Allen smiled. "I guess so. It may be the only chance you'll ever have to keep a horse. Of course, Mr. Wright still may decide not to do it."

Patty jumped up and hugged her mother. "Oh, thank you, thank you," she yelped. "I'll call Mr. Wright this minute."

It was David that answered the phone. He sounded almost as excited as Patty when he heard the news. "I'll tell Dad about it right away," he promised. "We can talk more about it tomorrow."

* * * * * *

The next day was Sunday, so Patty went to church and ate lunch with her mom. But, she was at the stable as soon as possible. She went right to Count's stall to tell him about her plan. The swelling in his chest was better. He quickly took a carrot from her.

"Dad is pretty happy about having a place for Count," said David as he jogged up. "He said we'll go see Mr. Roberts tonight."

"Good," cheered Patty. "I'll be so happy when all this is settled."

"Me too," Mr. Wright agreed. Patty hadn't seen

him step up behind David. "Do you think you will be able to keep Count's wound from getting full of dirt?"

"Oh, yes," beamed Patty. "I'll take good care of him."

"Will you go over to Mr. Roberts' with us tonight?" Mr. Wright continued. "Since he knows you, it might be better."

"Oh, sure," Patty agreed. "I think he'll open the door for me."

After supper, Patty and the Wrights climbed the steps to the spooky old house and knocked. "You had the guts to come over here by yourself before?" David whispered.

"Shhhh," said his father.

Mr. Roberts opened the door at the first knock. He looked better dressed than yesterday.

"I'm George Wright," said David's father, offering his hand. "I understand that you might let us keep a horse in your field for a while."

Mr. Roberts took Mr. Wright's hand, but his eyes were on Patty. "You'd better use the barn, too." he muttered. "Can't let the flies get to that wound."

"Yes, that's true," Mr. Wright agreed. "I'll be happy to pay you a reasonable . . ."

"Don't want money," the old man interrupted. "But, anytime this horse doesn't get good care, the deal is off."

"He'll get very good care," Mr. Wright assured him. "Patty will feed and water him twice a day. David and I will be checking on him, too."

Mr. Roberts nodded. "I'll be watching," he promised.

The next morning the Wrights brought Count in a big padded trailer. Patty was surprised when Mr. Roberts came out to watch the unloading. She

noticed his old eyes got misty when he saw the horse's ugly chest.

Count took one look at the long grass and began to eat.

Mr. Wright smiled and said, "I think he will heal quickly in such a nice place."

When they had gone, Mr. Roberts went back into his house. Patty carried water for the horse and tried to brush him while he grazed. Later, when the flies got bad, she decided to put him in the barn.

Patty tried to open several of the barn doors when Mr. Roberts came with a key. "The back door has a padlock," he told her.

When he had opened the back door, Patty was able to unhook all the other doors from inside. It was very dusty in the barn, so she opened some windows. Mr. Roberts brought a bale of straw for the stall and disappeared.

Count seemed to approve of the stall. He tried to eat the straw at first. But soon, he hung his head and went to sleep.

The next morning the vet came to look at Count. He was pleased with what he saw. "This is a great place for the horse," he said. "Mr. Wright should be able to sell him in about two months."

A few days later, Mr. Wright and David showed up. Patty ran to meet them. "Hi," she called. "I was wondering if you had forgotten us."

"It's been a very busy week," Mr. Wright told her.

"Yeah," added David. "We had to deliver all the horses and look for a new place to live."

"Did you find a place to live?" Patty asked eagerly.

"Yup," said David. "We're going to live at Hilltop. The new owner just hired Dad to take care of his mares and foals. Dad knows all about caring for horses."

Mr. Wright grinned. "Well, at least it's something I will enjoy doing," he explained.

"That's wonderful," Patty told them. Then she led the way to Count.

"He's looking good," Mr. Wright smiled. "The wound looks good and clean."

"The vet said you should be able to sell him in about two months," Patty answered sadly.

"Well, I suppose so," Mr. Wright said gently. "But, don't worry about that, yet. Just enjoy him while you can and keep up the good work."

Enjoy him while you can, Patty said to herself. That's what her mom had said when Patty had first met Count. How many times would she have to lose him? Would someone like Stacy come along to buy him after all that had happened?

Patty faithfully did her job and Count continued to improve. She noticed Mr. Roberts sometimes came out to pet the horse, but he rarely spoke to her.

One afternoon the Wrights came to see Count. There were huge grins on their faces. "We just sold this horse for a good price," David announced.

Patty gulped. She felt as if someone had kicked her in the stomach. Count wasn't completely healed. How could he be sold? "I can't give him up yet," she protested. Then she began to cry and headed for the house.

Before she went two steps, Mr. Wright grabbed her. "Patty, wait," he demanded. "Don't you want to know who bought the horse?"

Patty sobbed harder and shook her head. If it was someone like Stacy, I don't want to know about it, she said to herself.

"Well, I'm going to tell you," Mr. Wright insisted. "Count's new owner is our friend, Mr. Roberts."

Patty stopped crying and her mouth dropped open. "Mr. Roberts?" she gasped. "What is he going to do with the horse?"

David laughed, "Why don't you ask him yourself? He's headed this way."

Patty ran to the old man. "Mr. Roberts," she demanded. "What are you going to do with Count?"

The old man looked rather embarrassed. "I guess I fell in love with that horse just as you did. The only problem is that I'm too old to ride him. Do you know anyone that might do that for me?"

Patty sputtered, "Could I? Would you let me?"

The old man tried to look serious, but his eyes twinkled. "On only one condition," he said firmly.

"What's that?" Patty begged.

"That you take some riding lessons from Mr. Wright here. I'll pay for them, because I want the best for my new horse."

"Oh, wow," was all Patty could say. What else was there to say?

## About the Author

MARILYN D. ANDERSON grew up on a dairy farm in Minnesota. Her love for animals and her twenty-plus years of training and showing horses are reflected in many of her books.

A former music teacher, Marilyn has taught band and choir for seventeen years. She specialized in percussion and violin. She stays busy training young horses, riding in dressage shows, working at a library, giving piano lessons, and, of course, writing books.

Marilyn and her husband live in Bedford, Indiana.

Other books by Marilyn D. Anderson include *The Wild Arabian, I Don't Want a New Horse!* and *We Have to Get Rid of These Puppies!*